Coach Bob & Me

Author Catherine Gibson

Illustrations by Janice Hechter

For Children with Love Publications
Farmington, Connecticut
www.forchildrenwithlove.com

For Children With Love
P.O. Box 1552
Farmington, Connecticut 06034

Visit our website www.forchildrenwithlove.com

Printed in Singapore by Tien Wah Press [Pte] Limited
First Printing, January 2011

ISBN 978-0-9831221-0-4

To Bob Beltrandi
My dear friend and inspiration for this book.

To my sons, Tyler & Stefan

As I walked into the lunchroom at school one day, I noticed Coach Bob sitting at his usual table eating lunch. He liked sitting by the open window watching the kids play football. Sometimes the entire team would join him; everyone seemed to enjoy that, especially the Coach. Not just athletes, came to Coach Bob for advice. He was always willing to help anyone who needed it and he seemed to really care about the students.

He was well-respected, loved by his students and moved around so easily that people seemed to forget that he was in a wheelchair. At times, it made me feel sad to see him unable to walk. I often wondered what his life would be like if he hadn't had the accident. He never talked about it; he seemed content in spite of it.

There was a certain excitement about the arrival of fall, the wind blowing leaves around, the crisp air. People seemed to have so much more energy.

It was a beautiful autumn day and everyone wanted to play football, including me. I had never tried out for the team; I had never felt good enough to even try. Still, I enjoyed playing and managed to practice with others who, like me, weren't on the team.

There were some guys on the team who thought they were pretty cool, too cool. Once in awhile, in the hallway, they would intentionally bump into me while I was getting a book from my locker. As my papers spilled out onto the floor, they would laugh. I usually ate alone in the cafeteria and there were times when they would walk by my lunch table and nudge it, spilling my drink everywhere.

Although I wasn't on the team, there were a few of us who would go to the weight room during our free time and lift weights. I knew that football players should lift whenever they could to improve their strength. Most of the guys on the football team were stronger than me, but I didn't let that bother me. My brother, Tyler, encouraged me to use his weights and lift at home. I didn't feel very strong and didn't think I could lift much, but I still kept at it.

One afternoon, Coach came into the weight room to check on us. I think he could tell that I was trying my best and he was very encouraging. He told me he thought I was looking stronger, which was great to hear.

Our gym class, taught by the team's head coach, Coach Kelly, met on the track the following week. He told us we were going to be tested in three categories: running, distance jumping and on our lifting skills in the weight room. When we went back inside, I was surprised to see that there were only a couple of guys on the football team that could lift more weight than me. They seemed surprised to see what I could do and I felt pretty good about it.

The following day, I showed up early for lunch and was sitting alone. It was another perfect day for football. Coach Bob was early, too, and stopped by my table. "Great job yesterday, Stefan. Coach Kelly told me you've been working pretty hard in the weight room. Why don't you join us over at my table?"

"No thanks," I replied, adding, "I'm interested in this book about football and it's pretty good, so I don't mind sitting alone right now."

I showed him the book, which he looked at for a minute and said, "This is a great book, it looks like there are some good strategies in here. Tell you what, Stefan, once you've finished eating, why don't you bring the book over and show the guys?"

"Some of those guys are never very friendly to me Coach," I told him.

He seemed to understand and answered that they could be a bit overconfident at times, adding, "Well, keep plugging away, you're doing a great job. Join us after your lunch if you'd like."

Not long afterward, Coach Bob encouraged me to come over and sit at an empty seat at his table and told the team about my book. The coach took time to speak to us about the importance of good sportsmanship.

The next thing you know, Coach Bob had picked up my book and pointed out some plays that he wanted the team to practice.

As the week went by, I began to feel more like I belonged when I would see the guys from the team in the hallway between classes. They were friendlier toward me, gave me high fives or yelled out, "Hey, Stefan, how's it going?" My life seemed to have taken a turn for the better.

My mind continued to focus on how Coach's accident had changed his life. If only I was able to go back in time like they do in a movie or in a television program to change the outcome.

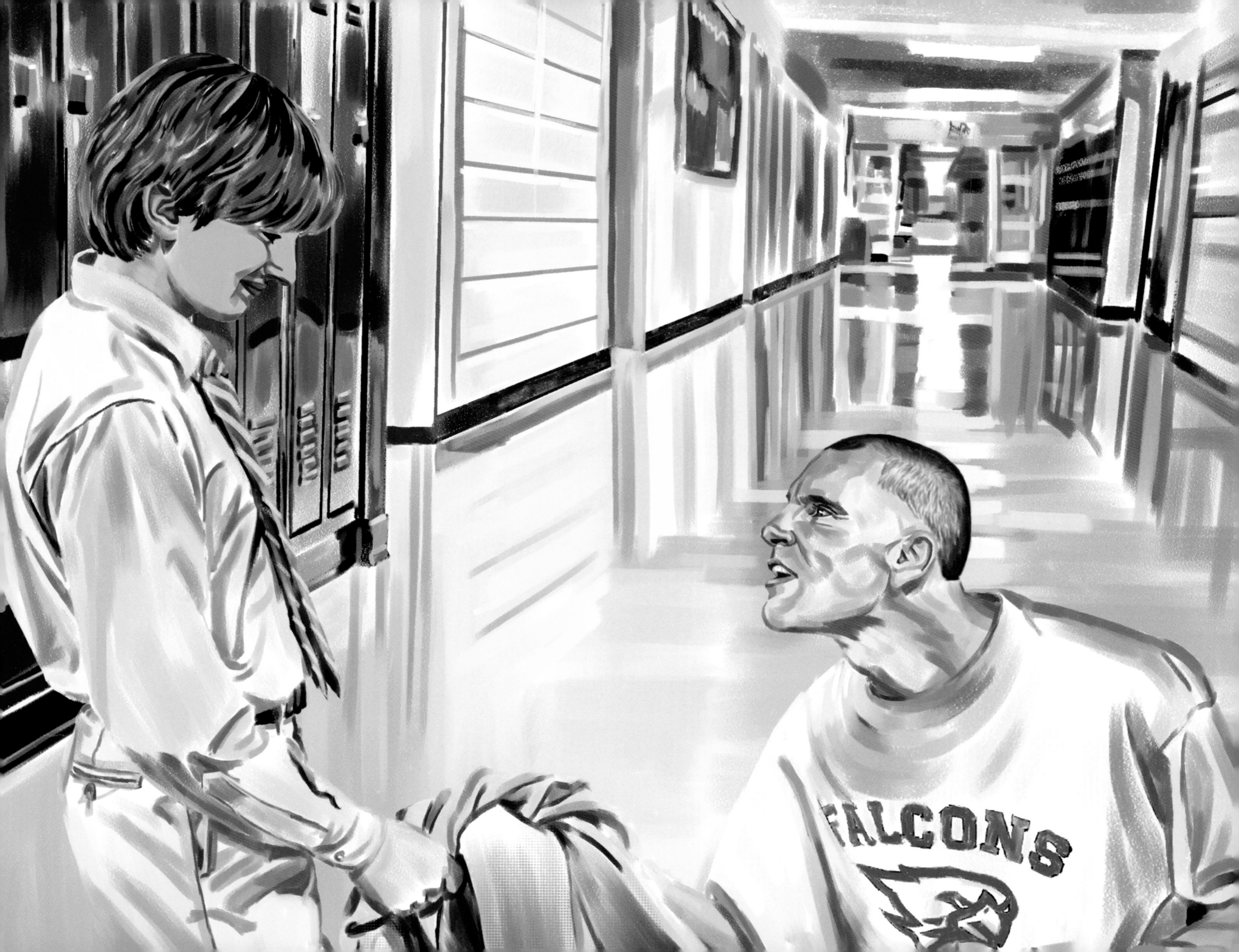

That Friday, Coach Bob came by my locker just before lunch. "Hey buddy, where've you been?" he asked with a smile. "I ordered team T-shirts and thought you might like one. Here's one, try it on." It felt pretty good and, best of all, it made me feel like I was part of the team.

Taking me aside, he asked, "What seems to be bugging you lately?" Quietly, I told him that I had been thinking about his accident and what his life would be like if it hadn't happened.

In a reassuring voice, he answered, "Thanks for your concern, Stefan, but I'm okay with it. When I was a young boy, I watched sports all the time and read everything that I could about sports. I always wanted to be a coach."

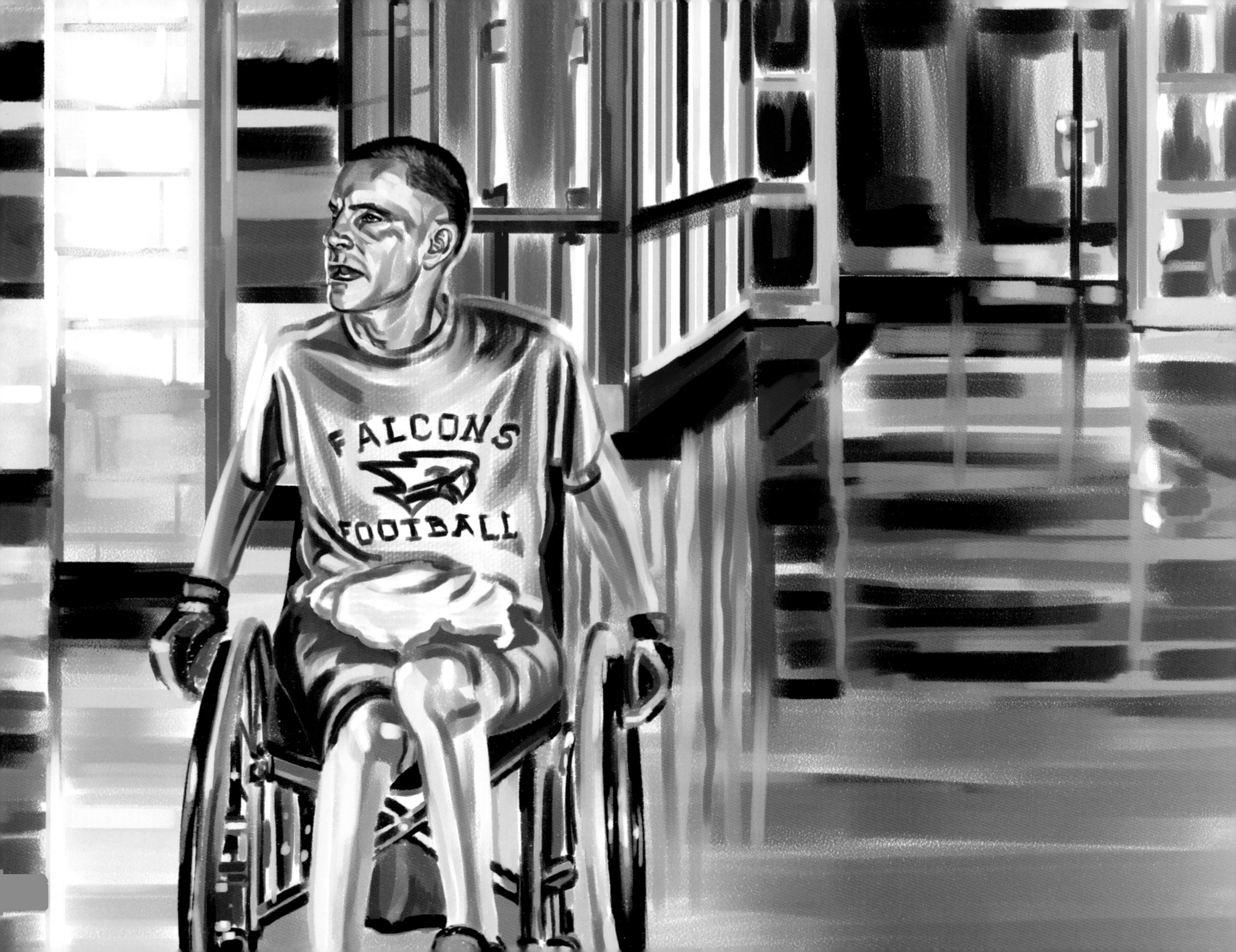

Coach Bob continued, "After my accident, I went through a tough time, but it made me focus on what I wanted to accomplish. I spent a lot of time in the hospital and realized it was more important than ever for me to be on the field, even if I was in a wheelchair. It made me want to work harder than ever to become a coach."

"I worked out a lot to improve my strength; I studied and learned all I could about coaching. Actually, I can get around pretty well. I bet I could wheel this chair faster than you think," he said, laughing.

"I know," I replied, "that thing can really move."

"Stefan, everyone has something they have to overcome. Remember back in the lunchroom when you thought that some of the guys were too tough? You were tougher than you thought and you have even overcome some of your shyness these last several weeks."

Coach added, "That is another example of strength. I'm proud of you, Stefan. You can do anything you want to, if you try hard enough. The truth is, I probably wouldn't be as good a coach now, if I hadn't had the accident. It made me more determined to do what I really wanted with my own life. After learning from my own experience, I am glad to help others."

"Thanks, for all the help you've given me, Coach. I notice that whenever you enter a room, there is either someone shouting out your name or giving you a pat on the back. You have so many friends!"

"That's true, Stefan. It proves that there's more to life than simply playing on a field.

That afternoon, we were on the field until it was nearly dark. Coach Bob made us take time out to notice the colorful sky." Always remember to take some time to look at the big picture in life," he reminded us.

Taking us by surprise, he switched gears and said, "Okay, let's get moving!" After a few more plays, I thought about how great it was to finally be part of a team.

The next morning, I grabbed my backpack and headed out the door to school. Thinking about the events of the last several weeks, I realized how my outlook on life had changed. Through Coach Bob's experience, I had learned that overcoming a challenge in life can help you identify your goals. I knew that whether we won the biggest game of the season or not wasn't important, it was knowing what you want and "going for it!"

Coach Bob believed in me and his friendship was the best part of all.

Photo by Victoria Freeman

About the Author

Catherine Czerwinski Gibson is a Connecticut native who has written two children's books prior to "Coach Bob & Me." Cathy's friendship with Bob Beltrandi began more than thirty years ago as high school students at East Catholic High School in Manchester, Connecticut. An accident as a young adult left Bob confined to a wheelchair. He is currently the assistant football coach at St. Paul's Catholic High School in Bristol, Connecticut.

Cathy's association with St. Paul's allowed her the opportunity to reconnect with Bob after many years. He inspired her to write this story and share with others the admiration and respect he has earned from students, parents and colleagues.

Public awareness of those with life challenges has become a necessary and important issue in today's world. Cathy conveys that message in her thoughtful stories about children with special gifts who are accepted for their individual strengths and winning personalities.

Cathy's award-winning first book, "Through Sophie's Eyes" received a medal at the Independent Publishers' Convention in New York City as well as a Mom's Choice Award. The soon-to-be-published sequel is titled, "Sophie Discovers Synchronized Swimming."

Her website is www.forchildrenwithlove.com

A portion of the proceeds from each book will be donated to local childrens causes.

About the Illustrator

Janice Hechter is a full-time children's book illustrator who enjoyed meeting Coach Bob and Stefan and was inspired by their story.

Janice is the illustrator of "Hooray for Heroes!" by Mollie Wilson and is currently illustrating her third book, "ABC of Discovery" by Lois Breitmeyer and Gladys Leithauser. She has been invited to numerous schools to guide students through the process of children's book illustration.

Janice resides in Farmington, Connecticut with her husband and daughter.

Her website is www.janicehechter.com